THE ODDYSSEY

FOR MORE **ODD** ADVENTURES,
CHECK OUT:

THE ODDyssey

BY **DAVID SLAVIN**

ILLUSTRATED BY
ADAM J. B. LANE

BASED ON CHARACTERS BY
DAVID SLAVIN
AND **DANIEL WEITZMAN**

HARPER
An Imprint of HarperCollinsPublishers

Library of Congress Control Number: 2019945992

ISBN 978-0-06-283955-8

Typography by Andrea Vandergrift

19 20 21 22 23   PC/LSCH   10 9 8 7 6 5 4 3 2 1

First Edition

CHAPTER 1

In case you haven't figured it out, it's my dad's birthday . . . and I haven't gotten him anything yet. You've been there, too, right? But you can't really blame me—I've got a lot of stuff going on!

1

HOMEWORK

AFTER-
SCHOOL
ACTIVITIES

TAKING CARE
OF MY DOG,
TRIANUS

Okay, maybe I don't have that much stuff going on. The truth is, my dad is harder to please than most dads. He's Zeus, the King of the Greek Gods.

Hey, I wonder if he'd like a drawing!

Hmmm.

And yes, you read that right: I'm *Oddonis*. Not *Adonis*. I'm the ODD version of a Greek God. Adonis is my twin brother. He's amazing and definitely NOT ODD. Also, unlike me, he's probably got something *way* over-the-top planned for my dad's birthday. This was his gift to Dad last year:

Yeah, I'm pretty sure I won't be able to slay a dragon in the next fifteen minutes. That's when my dad's party is supposed to start. Dad likes things HUGE—especially parties FOR HIM. But my mom, Freya, does not. She's Norwegian, and she thinks all you should get on your birthday is some fruitcake and someone to sing "Hurra for deg som fyller ditt år," this weird Norwegian birthday song that she loves.

Problem number one: Dad HATES Mom's fruitcake. Then again, does anybody actually like fruitcake? Worst. Cake. Ever! Oh, and here's an added bonus: my mom can't cook!

Problem number two: Dad's not big on the "Hurra for deg" song. And he *really* doesn't like doing the little dance Mom makes us all do when we sing it.

So that means Dad's got one birthday thing left that he actually likes: PRESENTS. Which I DON'T HAVE. I rifle through my closet, looking for something I can regift to him, but all I find is this so-called "sculpture" I did in art class years ago. It's made out of pasta, and even I can't tell what it's supposed to be!

But then a bolt of artistic inspiration hits me! I wrap a white handkerchief around the pasta and draw an inscription on the base!

BRILLIANT!

Okay, "brilliant" might be a little strong. But beggars can't be choosers, and the party's about to start! I put Ziti Zeus in the pocket of my toga and scoot downstairs.

CHAPTER 2

Aunt Demeter and Aunt Hestia are in the kitchen with my mom, helping her with the fruitcake. They're my dad's sisters. Aunt Demeter is the Goddess of grains. She always brings the flour for the cake.

Aunt Hestia is the Goddess of the hearth. She's keeping the fire going in the oven.

Too bad there's no Goddess of stuff that tastes good—because that's what my mom's fruitcake really needs!

"Hello, snuppa!" Mom says to me. "I'm about to take the fruitcake out, but I'm warning you: no sneaking a bite!"

"Oh, you don't have to worry about that, Mom," I say.

Aunt Hestia smiles at me, and Aunt Demeter gives me a wink.

"Couldn't he have just one little taste, Freya?" asks Aunt Demeter. "You know how Oddonis *loves* your fruitcake!"

"NO! It's Zeus's special day, and he gets the first piece! I'm sorry, Oddy."

I shoot my aunts a dirty look and try to keep from laughing. They're pretty cool, as aunts go. They're sweet and fun and easygoing—not at all like their brother (aka MY DAD). The relative who's most like my dad is my uncle Hades. Mom says that's why they don't get along! Dad and Uncle Hades have been in a feud for a long time. They used to be really close.

But over the years, they've grown apart. Dad kind of looks down on Hades. Then again, everyone looks down on Hades—because he's God of the Underworld! BA-DUMP-BUMP! Get it? *Down? Underworld?* Anyway, I have a lot of nice memories of my uncle.

Everyone says Hades is a little odd, and maybe that's why I've always liked him. I'm a little odd, too!

"Ta-da!" yells my mom. *"FRUKTKAKE!"* She pulls the fruitcake out of the oven, and it is . . .

"Beautiful!" says Aunt Hestia.

"It's your best one yet, Freya," echoes Aunt Demeter.

"Jippi!!!" Mom squeals. (That's Norwegian for "Yippee!!!") "Let the party begin! Oddy, you take your aunts into the living room and join your father."

Aunt Hestia and Aunt Demeter put their arms around me, and we walk out of the kitchen.

"You don't really think that cake is beautiful, do you?" I whisper.

"Oh my Gods, no," replies Aunt Hestia. "I tried to burn it!"

"I'd rather eat a bale of hay," mutters Aunt Demeter. "But it makes your mom happy, so that makes us happy!"

"Plus, your dad has to act like he loves it!" chuckles Aunt Hestia.

"That's the best part!" says Aunt Demeter. "I mean, other than watching him do that silly birthday dance!"

"What are you two cackling about?" Dad asks as we sit down.

"Oh, nothing, birthday boy," giggles Aunt Demeter. "Just waiting for your special cake!"

"Ugh," groans my dad. "*Fruitcake* again?"

"We can't spoil the surprise!" says Aunt Hestia. "But it's your *favorite*!"

"Great," Dad grumbles. "Speaking of favorites— Oddonis, where's your brother?"

TELL ME HE DIDN'T JUST SAY THAT.

"Beats me," I reply grumpily. "He left early this morning."

"Well, I certainly hope he hasn't forgotten my birthday!"

"Not much chance of that, Dad," I say.

I wanted to say, "Oh, please, Dad, Adonis never misses a chance to show off," but I thought I'd be nice.

Then I hear a loud BANG! The front door crashes open, and in walks—make that, in *rides*—my brother, Adonis . . . on top of a giant bull!

CHAPTER 3

"HAPPY BIRTHDAY, O GREAT AND POWER-FUL FATHER!" thunders Adonis. "I bring to you the Cretan Bull! Pretty cool, huh?"

"Well, well!" roars Dad. "Adonis, you've done it again!"

(My Ziti Zeus is looking even sadder now.)

"He put up a good fight," says Adonis. "But he was no match for me. Oh, and Heracles helped a little, too."

Heracles helped *a little*? If I know my brother, this is how it all went down:

"Very impressive, Adonis!" says Dad. "Freya, come see what Adonis got me for my birthday!"

Mom walks in, takes one look at the bull, and shrieks, "UFF DA! OKSE!!! GET THAT THING OUT OF MY HOUSE!"

"But it's the Cretan Bull!" grouses Dad. "And it's my birthday!"

"Oh, all right," says Mom. "But *only* because it's your birthday. Heracles, put the cow in the corner."

"Okay, Mrs. Z," says Heracles.

"Time for fruktkake and 'Hurra for deg!'" Mom chirps.

"Time for MORE PRESENTS!" Dad responds. "Bestow thy gifts unto me!"

Aunt Hestia gives Dad a fire stick. And I mean . . . *an actual stick of fire!*

"A fire stick!" yells Adonis. "Can I play with it, Dad?"

"Let me think about that," says Dad. "Umm . . . NO!"

Then Aunt Demeter gives him a bushel of wheat. (That's what she *always* gives.)

"You can play with this, Adonis," says Dad, handing him the bushel.

Hmmm. Maybe Dad won't mind Ziti Zeus after all! It can't be any worse than getting wheat!

"Well, I'd like to thank my *sisters* for being here," says Dad, "and for giving me these gifts. Of course, my BROTHER didn't show . . . *again.*"

15

"I think he's still hurt that you didn't go to his birthday party," says Aunt Demeter.

"*Me?* Go to *his* party? Hello! I am ZEUS, King of the Gods! I've got a lot of stuff going on!"

"Oh, really?" says Mom.

"Besides, I *hate* the Underworld," Dad sneers. "It's dark and depressing and scary. Who cares if my brother lives there? I'm king of the whole world, and if I don't want to go somewhere, I don't have to go! So there!!!"

I really wish I didn't wait to go last to give my dad

his gift. I should've given him Ziti Zeus during the *five seconds* when he was actually in a good mood! But I can't put this off any longer. I reach into my pocket and pull out . . . a letter. *A letter?* How'd that get in there???

CHAPTER 4

Oddonis,
I think we both know that Ziti Zeus doesn't cut it as a present. Give this poem to your dad instead. Consider it my gift!

—Uncle Hades

Whaaaaaat? Howwwww?

"Oddonis?" says Dad. "Are you okay?"

I am definitely NOT okay. I am TOTALLY freaking out! Ziti Zeus is GONE and now I have NOTHING and I'm DESPERATE, so I say, "Uhh . . . yeah! I'm . . . just . . . getting your present."

"Oooh! Really? What is it?"

"It's . . . a poem?"

18

"A poem!" says Dad. "I *love* poems! Especially when they're about ME!"

"Greaaaat," I say, handing the letter to my dad. "Here you go."

Dad clears his throat and reads out loud.

Dearest Zeus, the mighty king,
To you we hail and praise and sing!
And for your happy birthday gift,
You'll hereby make this boyish shift,
From here on out, a child you'll be,
And act as though you're only three!

All of a sudden, there's a bolt of lightning and a clap of thunder . . . *inside our house!* Smoke fills the room, the Cretan Bull snorts, and my aunts (and

Adonis) scream. What the heck is going on here???
It's TOTAL CHAOS!

My mom yells, "Is everyone okay?"

"Yes!" reply my aunts.

"Yeah!" add Adonis and Heracles and me.

"Zeus?" asks Mom.

Nothing.

"Zeus?" she asks again. "Are you all right?"

As the smoke starts to clear, I see my dad sitting right where he was before. The only difference is that his toga is now wrapped around his waist like a diaper. He looks up at everyone, pounds his fists on his thighs, and cries, "*WAAAHHH! ZEUSY WANT MORE PRESENTS! ZEUSY WANT MORE PRESENTS!!!! WAAAAAAAAAAAHHHHHHHHHH!!!!!!!!*"

"What did you do now, Oddy?" sneers my brother.

"I didn't do anything!" I say. (Did I???)

"Well, you must've done *something*," replies Adonis. "Look at Dad!"

"That was some poem you wrote, Oddonis," says Aunt Hestia.

"But I didn't write it! I swear!"

"Oddonis, you know how I feel about lying," Mom says, her voice rising with anger. "You *said* it was your poem. He *read* your poem. And now your poem has turned your father into *A TODDLER*!!!"

"Ooooh! Mommy mad!" says Dad.

"I'm not your mommy!" yells Mom.

"NOT MY MOMMMMMMY???" cries Dad. "WAAAAAAAAAAAHHHHHHH!!!!!"

"I think he needs his mommy, Freya," says Aunt Demeter.

"I think he needs a nap," says Aunt Hestia.

That gets Dad's attention.

"Zeusy have nappy wappy! Zeusy go sleepy poopy!"

"Oh, all right." Mom sighs. "I'll take 'Zeusy' upstairs. And when I come down, you better have a good explanation for this, Oddonis."

"Oooooh! Oddy Woddy in twoooublllle!"

Zeusy's right. Oddy Woddy is definitely in twouble wouble!!!

CHAPTER 5

Waiting for Mom to come downstairs feels like . . .

And Adonis staring at me and doing *THIS* sure isn't helping!

Finally Mom walks in and announces, "Zeus, son of Cronus and Rhea, King of the Gods and ruler of all Olympus, is taking a nappy wappy." Then she turns to me and says, "All right, Oddonis, out with it."

I take a big gulp and confess. (Warning: there's some crying involved.)

"Okay, I didn't get Dad a present because I put it off to the last minute and then I couldn't think of anything so I made Ziti Zeus and then Adonis came in with that bull and Aunt Hestia had the fire stick and then Aunt Demeter gave Dad that lame-o wheat and I thought whoa this is my chance so I went to get Ziti Zeus but he wasn't there and that's when I found

Uncle Hades's poem and I didn't have anything so I pretended it was my poem and I don't know what happened after that but now Dad's a baby and it's all my fault and I'm so so sorry! *Waaaaaahhhhhhhh!!!!!*"

"Maybe Oddy needs a nappy wappy, too," grumbles Adonis.

Thankfully, Mom gives me a big hug and says, "I don't understand half of what you just said, kjære, but I believe you." She looks at Uncle Hades's letter and passes it to my aunts.

"It's Hades's writing, all right," says Aunt Demeter.

"I didn't know he was *that* mad at Zeus," says Aunt Hestia.

"Can you reverse the spell?" asks Mom.

"We can't," replies Aunt Hestia. "Only Hades can."

"Well, somebody needs to talk to him," says Mom. "And soon! I hate to say this about my own husband, but baby Zeusy is a brat!"

"I don't know how much good it'll do, but we can try," says Aunt Demeter.

"You better go now," orders Mom. "Zeusy's nap won't last forever!"

We hug Hestia and Demeter goodbye and wish them luck. And lucky for us, Mom gives them the fruitcake, too!

"Listen up, you two," Mom says to Adonis and me. "Gather all the baby stuff from the basement and think of ways to entertain your father when he wakes up. I'll start preparing his lunch. Go!"

"You're making way too big a deal out of this, Mom," I protest. "So Dad's a little kid now. How hard can it be to take care of him?"

Just then, we hear a voice wailing from upstairs.

"UH-OH! ZEUS Y JUST WENT BIG POTTY!!!"

"I'll let you take care of that," Mom says to me.

CHAPTER 6

Okay, I'm not going to talk about the potty thing—EVER—but after that, Zeusy was actually a lot of fun!

See, my dad's never been much of a *player* . . . not with me, at least. Full disclosure, though: I've always had trouble playing games, too.

But now that Dad's a junior Zeus, he seems to really like hanging out with me!

Zeusy is still asleep the next morning when Adonis and I leave for school. Mom's worried about having to take care of Dad the whole day, but she's *super*-worried that word will get out about Dad's "situation." She even makes us pinkie swear that we won't tell anybody!

"I'm serious as a hjerteinfarkt," Mom says. (That's "heart attack" in Norwegian.) "No one can find out about your father. And I mean NO ONE."

"Okay, okay," says Adonis. "But why?"

"If the other Gods discover their king is now an infant, they'll be all over Olympus faster than a loppe on a hund!" (That's "a flea on a dog.")

Full disclosure: I'm *terrible* at keeping secrets, so I'm a nervous wreck at school. It's weird not being able to talk to my friends about my dad, but pinkie swearing is serious business! I try to stay cool, but it's possible I seem a *little* on edge. First, on the school chariot . . .

Then, in the lunchroom . . .

"What is with you?" asks my friend Mathena.

"I DON'T KNOW WHAT YOU'RE TALKING ABOUT!" I say, realizing that I'm actually screaming. "I'M FINE!"

"If you say so," replies Gaseous. "So, how was your dad's birthday?"

"WHY DO YOU ASK THAT?????"

"Umm . . . because it was your dad's birthday yesterday?"

"WAS NOT!"

"But you told us you were having a birthday party for him," says Mathena.

"NO! NO! NO BIRTHDAY! NO PARTY! NO NOTHING!!!"

Just then, Adonis and Heracles pass by our table.

Hmmm.

This is going to be harder than I thought!

CHAPTER 7

I'm so afraid of spilling the beans that I purposely skip taking the bus after school. I run all the way home, and as soon as I open the door and see my mom, I can tell what kind of day it's been.

"Can't . . . take it . . . anymore . . . ," she mumbles.
"Where's Dad?" I ask.

"In your room," she replies. "That's the only way I could calm him down."

"Okay, I'll go up and see him."

"I'm sorry, Oddy."

"What are you sorry for?" I ask.

"You'll see."

Uh-oh.

"NOOOOOO!!! STOP, ZEUSY! BAD ZEUSY!"
I'm so mad at Zeusy that I actually do *this*!

But he looks so sad, so ashamed . . . and so cute!
I just can't stay mad at him!

OMGs! What is happening to me? Am I becoming . . . a *parent*?

CHAPTER 8

The next morning, Mom looks even worse than the day before. Meanwhile, Dad is sitting happily in his high chair, rubbing oatmeal in his hair.

"I had to get up five different times in the night," Mom whispers. "Your father kept wanting a drink of water!"

"That's a lot of water," I say. "I'm surprised he made it through without—"

37

"He didn't." Mom sighs.

"Zeusy make pee-pee in his beddy-bye!" shouts Dad.

"I'm so tired—I don't think I can handle another day alone with him," says Mom. "Can one of you stay home? I'll write you a note!"

"I've got a test," Adonis says quickly.

ACTUAL "TEST"

"I—I—I've got a test, too," I stammer.

ACTUAL "TEST"

"Oh, all right." Mom sighs. "But get home as fast as you can!"

On our way to the school chariot, I say to Adonis, "I think today will be better than yesterday for Mom. Maybe she and Zeusy will have some fun!"

"'Maybe she and Zeusy will have some fun!'" mimics Adonis. "Zeusy, Zeusy, Zeusy! Why don't you just marry Zeusy?"

"That doesn't even make sense!"

"Boy, I thought I'd seen it all when you lucked into being class co-president," gripes Adonis. "But now this spell you cast has lucked you into being Dad's pet!"

"Umm . . . actually, I won that election and asked you to be my co-president," I reply.

"Wow, thanks for rubbing it in my face. Really nice, sore winner!"

"Wait, you're the one who—"

"Next I suppose you're going to say that Dad loves you more!"

"I never said—!"

"Unbelievable, *backstabbro*," sneers Adonis. "I knew you were odd, but who knew you were *cruel*, too?"

Arrgghhh! Adonis has been Dad's favorite for, like . . . FOREVER! I get ONE DAY of Dad liking me and now *I'm* the bad guy??? I shake my head nonstop at school, and I'm still shaking it on my way back home! (I've also got a terrible headache, for some reason.)

I try to put Adonis out of my mind and think happier thoughts—like how I'll get to hang with my buddy Zeusy again! I missed the big/little guy! I'm crossing my fingers that he and Mom had a drama-free day together, but then I get home and see this . . .

Oh, no. I run upstairs, yelling, "Mom? Zeusy? Anybody???"

No answer. I run back down to take a look in the living room. I find Mom sprawled out on the couch, fast asleep!

"MOM!" I shout, startling her awake. "MOM!"

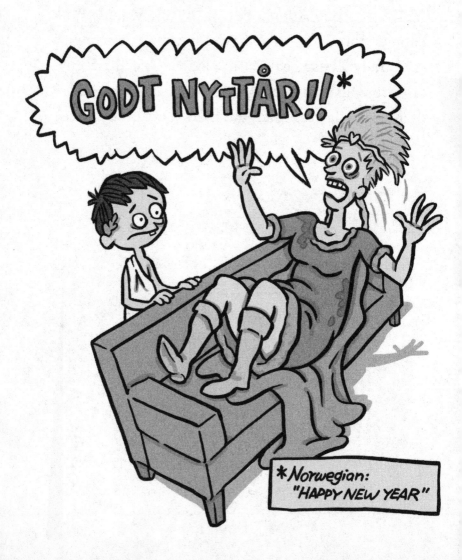

GODT NYTTÅR!!*

*Norwegian: "HAPPY NEW YEAR"

"Mom, where's Zeusy?" I scream. "Where's Zeusy???"

"He was right here a minute ago!" Mom replies.

"Well, he's gone now!" I say.

"Oh nei oh nei!" Mom screams. "We have to find him!"

We bolt for the door and stop dead in our tracks. Why?

We notice Dad's box of lightning bolts is open . . . and empty! And crumpled up on the floor, we see this!

Just then, Adonis enters and says, "What's up?"

"I'll tell you what's up," I reply. "Zeusy's on the loose, and maybe . . . in the nude!"

CHAPTER 9

The three of us head out in search of PNZ (Probably Naked Zeusy). We scour the whole neighborhood but can't find him anywhere.

"We have to keep looking," Mom says. "The Gods can never know what's happened to your father!"

"Well, I'm going back to the house first," says Adonis.

"Why?" I ask.

"Duh! To get an umbrella, dummy. It's gonna pour."

What is he talking about? It's a gorgeous sunny day!

"Honning, have you had too much sun?" asks Mom. "It's beautiful out!"

"Oh, yeah?" replies Adonis. "Look over there!"

Hmmm.

"Wow," I say. "That's some seriously bad weather."

"That's not weather!" shrieks Mom. "That's your father! Let's go!"

Together we hightail it up into the hills. "You already know about your father and his lightning bolts, but there's so much more he can do," Mom explains. "Because he's God of the sky, he can make weather: floods, hurricanes, blizzards, all kinds of storms."

"Can I do that?" asks Adonis.

"Nope. Sorry."

"What a rip-off!" pouts Adonis.

(I'm certainly not going to ask if *I* can make weather. I can't even make toast!)

As we get closer, it starts raining really hard! In the distance, we can hear Zeusy giggling and yelling, "BOOM! BOOM! BOOM!"

We hide behind a big rock for safety. I turn to Mom and Adonis and whisper, "What do we do?"

"Easy!" hisses Adonis. "We rush in and grab him!"

"Maybe we can talk to him," I say. "You know—*reason* with him!"

"No," declares Mom. "There's only one thing that stops a tempestuous toddler. Stand back, boys. It's *Thunder Mother time.*"

Mom shakes out her arms and cracks her neck

like a boxer getting ready for a big fight. She closes her eyes, clears her throat, and this . . . *sound* . . . emerges from the deepest part of her being. It starts in her toes, rises up through her belly, and ROARS from her mouth. OMGs! Adonis and I know that sound all too well. Our eyes bug out, and the hairs on our necks stand straight up. We grab each other and hold on for dear life. We're scared to death—and she's not even thundering at us!

Zeusy freezes. He drops the lightning bolt and tornado he was playing with, and tries to locate where that *horrible* noise just came from. Mom steps out from behind the rock and starts walking toward him, very slowly and deliberately.

"Who's been a bad God?" Mom mutters in her lowest, quietest, most disapproving voice.

"Zeusy?" asks Zeusy, like he hopes he's wrong.

"That's right," she continues. "Zeusy's been a bad God. And what happens to bad Gods?"

"Dey . . . dey . . . dey," stammers Zeusy. "Dey—"

"THEY GET PUNISHED, THAT'S WHAT!" screams Adonis.

Zeusy's eyes open wider—and *POOF!*—the next thing you know, he's . . . GONE!

CHAPTER 10

"**O**ops," says Adonis. "My bad."

"You're darn right, your bad!" snaps Mom. "He could be anywhere now. Or . . . any*thing*!"

"What do you mean—any*thing*?" I ask.

"Your father has another power that I didn't tell you about." Mom sighs. "He can shape-shift!"

"Shape-shift?" I ask. "What's that?"

"That means he can turn himself into whatever he wants by just thinking it!"

"Can I do that?" asks Adonis.

"No!" barks Mom.

"Double rip-off!" pouts Adonis.

"That's crazy!" I say. "He can transform himself into anything?"

"Bingo," replies Mom. (That's "bingo" in Norwegian. Oh, wait . . .)

"So what are we supposed to do?" asks Adonis.

"Keep looking," says Mom. "And ask yourselves, 'If Zeusy could go anywhere and be anything, where would Zeusy go and what would Zeusy be?'"

"I'm beat," says Adonis.

"And I'm stumped," says Mom. "He could be any-where. I hate to say it, but I think we're licked."

"We're not licked yet," I say. "But Zeusy will be! Follow me!"

Why didn't I think of it before? We race to every kid's dream destination: Mount Olycious Ice Cream! IT'S AMAZING! Eighty-five flavors! All the top-pings you could ever want! And the world's biggest sundae: the Gigantes! That's thirty-six pints of ice cream, five quarts of toppings, whipped cream, nuts, and cherries, all served in a golden chariot!

"Can I help you?" asks the girl behind the counter.

"One Gigantes, please," I say.

"A *Gigantes*???" groans Mom. "Oh, Oddy, no!"

"Trust me, Mom," I reply. "Now, what flavors do we want? I like vanilla."

"Eighty-five flavors and you want VANILLA?" mocks Adonis. "You're even odd when it comes to ice cream!"

I ask Mom what she wants, and she says to the guy, "Let's see. Do you have sjokoladekuler?"

"No."

"Kransekakestenger?"

"No."

"Ingefærnøtter? Tilslørte bondepiker? Havreflarn?"

"No. No. And . . . seriously, yuck."

"What kind of ice cream parlor is this???" she cries.

"Mom, the question is . . . what kind of ice cream does *Zeusy* like?" I ask.

"Oh, that's easy," she says. "He only likes Neapolitan Greek frozen yogurt."

"That's like, the worst old-dude dessert ever!" moans Adonis.

For once I agree with my brother. But desperate times call for desperate flavors!

"I don't get it," says Adonis as we lift the Gigantes onto our shoulders and carry it over to the nearest table. "Does this mean we're giving up trying to find Zeusy?"

"Not at all," I reply. "Just wait and see."

CHAPTER 11

Zeusy wins the battle against the Gigantes . . .

But loses the war.

After Zeusy finally falls asleep, we hear voices downstairs. Mom and Adonis and I run down to see who's there. It's Aunt Hestia and Aunt Demeter!

"How'd it go?" I ask.

"Umm . . . ," says Aunt Demeter. "Can we talk in the den? It's been a hard couple of days."

I guess it's been a hard couple of days for everyone! We head into the den and sit down together.

"So? What's the news?" asks Mom worriedly.

"Not good, I'm afraid." Hestia sighs.

"Hades wouldn't listen to us," adds Demeter. "He says Zeus has always been a baby and that he should *stay* a baby."

"That's it???" says Mom. "I'm supposed to just accept this? What about my marriage? What about my children? What about Olympus?"

"There might be a way," Hestia says. "But—"

"Why bring that up, Hestia?" interrupts Demeter. "It's impossible!"

"What is?" asks Mom. "What are you not telling me?"

"Hades said that he *might* reverse the spell if someone else visited the Underworld," says Hestia.

"Who?" Mom demands. "Me?"

"Not you," says Demeter. "Oddonis."

She hands me a postcard.

CHAPTER 12

Me? Go to the *Underworld*??? I just started taking the school chariot by myself last year!

"Oddy looks like he's gonna throw up!" says Adonis.

"I'm okay," I say, trying not to throw up. "I'm just thinking, why does everyone have to be mad at each other all the time?"

"Hey, we're Gods," states Adonis. "We fight. That's what we do. And like it or not, that's what we'll always do."

Well, I *don't* like it, I think to myself. I've NEVER liked it. I only wish I could DO something about it—I mean, other than going to the Underworld!

Then, all of a sudden, out of nowhere, my legs start standing up!

What the—? It's like there's a war going on inside me!

"Uhh . . . I guess . . . umm . . . since I'm the one who helped put the spell on Dad, then I'm the one who should go to the . . . Un . . . Un . . . Un . . ."

". . . Underworld."

"No, no, no, kjære," says Mom. "I won't let you. It's too dangerous."

"You heard Aunt Hestia and Aunt Demeter, Mom. We don't have a choice. Besides, I love having a little brother, but not when he's also my dad!"

"Are you sure, Oddy?" asks Aunt Hestia.

"OF COURSE I'M NOT SURE!" I say, much louder than I'd intended. "But you guys all have to stay and watch Zeusy. This is the only way, right?"

"I'm afraid so," says Aunt Demeter.

"Well, you're certainly not going *alone*," proclaims Mom.

"NO WAY!" crows a voice from behind me. Wait—who crowed that?

"Oddy's not going to the Underworld without me!" Adonis declares.

Wow. Could it be that my brother actually cares?

"He's not getting all the glory," says Adonis. "If anybody's going to save the day, it's me! *I'm* the hero here—not him!"

Hmmm. Guess not.

CHAPTER 13

Mom gives Adonis and me our marching orders: find a crew and bring them back to our house for a top secret meeting. We can each take two friends with us on our journey. It's pretty easy to guess who Adonis is going to ask: his two best buds.

I have to admit, they're not the worst choices in the world. We're traveling by boat, and Poseidon *is*

God of the oceans. And we're going to need someone to row, row, row the boat, and Heracles is strong
as an ox!

Make that stronger than an ox!

As for me, picking a crew is a bit more . . . complicated. I've got four choices.

Make that three choices! We can't afford to get sick on our journey, and Germes is walking, talking pneumonia!

I've gotta take Gaseous because he's my BFF.

And I think it would be really smart to ask Mathena. See, we've got a lot of *brawn* on the boat, but we're a little shy on *brains*.

So, I know what I need to do: NOT TELL PUNEOUS. (And yes, I also know I'm a TOTAL COWARD for doing that.)

I find Gaseous and Mathena and invite them to the meeting. They're confused but intrigued. They agree to follow me back home, and as we're walking, a part of me is actually getting a little excited about this odyssey. It's a kids-only road trip! I mean, except for the "adult supervisor" Mom insists that we have. And even that should be okay! Adonis and I each told Mom who we'd like our supervisor to be. Here's Adonis's choice:

ADONIS'S CHOICE:
COACH GLUTEUS
MAXIMUS
KINDA COOL. MAKES EVERYONE
DO PUSH-UPS, THOUGH!

And here's my choice:

MY CHOICE:
FRYONYSUS
TOTALLY COOL. MAKES
AWESOME PANCAKES!

When we walk into the house, though, we see
Mom made *her own choice.*

PRINCIPAL
DEADIPUS?
UNCOOL. MAKES WEIRD
CREAKING NOISES. SMELLS
LIKE COBWEBS AND COUGH
DROPS.

Awwww—come on, Mom! But there's no time to complain. As soon as everyone's settled, Mom calls the top secret meeting to order.

"You are all here on a matter of utmost urgency," she says. "Recently, a spell was cast on my husband, and our dear leader, Zeus—"

"By Oddonis," Adonis interrupts.

"Mom!" I protest.

"The spell was cast by *Hades*, Zeus's brother—"

"And was delivered by Oddonis," Adonis says.

"MO-OM!" I whine.

"By *mistake*," Mom continues. "And we need your help to break the spell."

"I'm in," says Gaseous. "As long as I don't have to go to the Underworld."

"You have to go to the Underworld," Mom replies.

Mom turns to Deadipus. "Principal Deadipus, I have chosen you to watch over these children. And I need you to convince the school that this is an *educational* field trip. We cannot reveal the true reason for this journey."

Then Mom turns to our friends. "You are my sons' closest allies—the ones Adonis and Oddonis trust most to join them on this quest. I thank you."

"Forgive me, Freya," says Principal Deadipus. "But you still haven't told us *why* we are going. What was the spell? What is the matter with our beloved Zeus?"

"I'll show you," says Mom. "But you are all sworn to secrecy. Even if you choose not to go, you must swear to tell *no one* what you are about to see."

"We swear," everyone swears.

"Hestia? Demeter?" Mom calls. "Bring Zeusy in, please."

Aunt Hestia and Aunt Demeter enter the den, holding Dad's hands.

"Zeusy, say hello to our guests," says Mom.

Zeusy waves and screams, "HI!!!" to everyone . . . except Principal Deadipus.

AAAAH!
HE SCARY!

"It's okay!" I whisper to Dad. Then I try my best to think like a three-year-old. "That's . . . Zeusy's friend . . . Mister Boneypoo!"

"HAHAHAHAHAHA! BONEYPOO!" screams Dad with delight.

Mom says, "Does that answer your question, Principal *Boneypoo*?"

"It does indeed, madam," replies Principal Dead-ipus.

Zeusy spots Clucky and Ducky sitting next to Mathena, claps his hands together and yells, "Play Duck, Duck, Goose! Play Duck, Duck, Goose now!!!!"

As the rest of us join the almighty ruler of Mount Olympus in a game of Duck, Duck, Goose, the grown-ups make plans.

CHAPTER 14

We're all set to go. As Heracles single-handedly loads supplies onto the boat, Principal Deadipus calls the roll.

"Adonis?"

"Here!"

"Oddonis?"

"Umm . . . I guess so?"

"Poseidon?"

"Ahoy!"

"Heracles?"

"There! Me mean, here!"

"Gaseous?"

Pffffffffffffffffffffftttttttttttt!!!!

"A simple 'here' would have sufficed, Gaseous," scolds Deadipus. "Mathena?"

"Present and accounted for, sir!"

"Clucky and Ducky?"

"Buck buck buck!"

"Quack quack quack!"

"Trianus?"

"Woof!"

"Good! Am I missing anyone?" asks Deadipus.

"Puneous! Here!"

I turn, look down, and sure enough, there's Puneous!

"We're going, and you can't stop us!" says Puneous.

"I'm sorry, Puneous," says Principal Deadipus. "You obviously didn't read the sign."

"Rats!!!" wails Puneous.

Mom is there to say goodbye to us. Dad's at home with Aunt Hestia and Aunt Demeter because Mom's sure Zeusy would have made a scene if he'd come. And speaking of making a scene, I hope Mom doesn't start to cry, because whenever *she* cries, *I* cry, too—and I don't want to bawl in front of everybody!

"Give these acorns to the entire crew," Mom instructs Adonis and me. "They'll keep you safe. And the two of you, take these trolls for good luck!"

"Be good to each other, *for once*, my elsklings," Mom says. "Adonis, watch out for your brother, and Oddonis, you do the same. Take care of each other, and . . . and . . . *sniff sniff* . . ."

"DON'T DO IT, MOM!"

". . . come home to your mamma, safe and sound!"

Mom starts crying. That does it. The floodgates open. I start wailing, but when I look up, I don't feel so bad.

I guess nobody likes to see a mother cry! Still sniffling, we walk up the gangplank and climb aboard the *Greek Freak*. Our helmsman greets us.

"I'm Phaethon, your helmsman," he mutters mournfully. "My father is Helios, the Sun God. He granted me one wish, and I asked to drive his sun chariot across the sky. He said it would be too much for me. I said it wouldn't be, but it was, and I crashed. As punishment, I'm doomed to drive a school chariot for all eternity. And now, I must drive this boat to the Underworld. Anchors aweigh."

Hey, he's the only driver we could find!

We trim the mainsail, lower the boom, and batten down the hatches. (Okay, I have no idea what any of that stuff means—I just pretend to.) Heracles starts rowing, and the next thing you know, we've set sail.

We're barely out of the harbor, and already I'm a whole bunch of sicks: heartsick, homesick . . . and seasick!

CHAPTER 15

After a while, it's not so bad being out on the water. It's actually quite peaceful! Sunlight dances on the deep blue ocean, and salty breezes fill my lungs. The Underworld feels far, far away. Then, because it's almost impossible for me to be happy for too long, I suddenly realize that I have no idea where we're going! I find Poseidon and ask him to explain.

"Ya got me," says Poseidon.

"Don't you know?" I say. "You *are* God of the oceans."

"Look around, dude," he says. "The oceans are *huge*. You expect me to know every last inch of them? Do you know all the weirdos in the world?"

"Then . . . how will we figure out where we're going?"

"Ask Phaethon—he's got the map."

I head up to our trusty helmsman and decide to flip the script on him. "You're Phaethon, our helmsman," I say. "Your father is Helios, the Sun God.

He granted you one wish, yada yada yada, I got it."

Phaethon looks shocked. "I . . . I . . . I'm Phaethon."

"Right. So, Phaethon, do you have the map to the Underworld?"

"It's in that basket there. I'm Phaethon, your helmsman."

I reach for the large, rolled-up map and spread it out in front of me. I'm pretty shocked by what I see.

WHAT THE WHAT???

"Wow, that's bad," murmurs Phaethon. "Almost as bad as crashing your father's sun chariot—"

"What happened to the map, Phaethon???" I say.

"Beats me," replies Phaethon. "It's been sitting in that basket the whole time."

I look down into the basket. I'm pretty shocked by what I see, PART TWO!

Bruiser! That stupid hamster stowed away and ate our map! Then it hits me. "If you're here," I say to the ravenous rodent, "then I know who else is, too!" I grab Bruiser and start searching. I reach the lifeboat hanging off the back of the ship and throw open the cover.

"I told you no one could stop us," says Puneous. "Oh, and I'll tell you one more thing: if I don't get out of this lifeboat soon, I'm going to HEAVE HO!"

CHAPTER 16

When the rest of the crew hears that Puneous stowed away—and then sees what his boy Bruiser did to the map—a number of options are considered.

Principal Deadipus steps in and takes charge.

"Calm yourselves, children! Let us examine the situation before jumping to any conclusions. Now, it is true that a portion of our map has been lost—"

"You mean eaten!" says Adonis. "By a rat!"

"*But* I am sure we have other options at our disposal. Poseidon, you are king of the oceans. Do you know how to guide us to the Underworld?"

"Nope," says Poseidon.

"Very well. Phaethon, you are our helmsman. Do you know how to guide us to the Underworld?"

"Nope," says Phaethon.

"I see. Then I believe it is safe to assume that . . . WE ARE DOOMED!!!"

"Principal Deadipus," interjects Mathena.

"WOE IS ME!!!"

"PRINCIPAL DEADIPUS!" screams Mathena.

"WHAT IS IT, MATHENA???"

"I can guide us to the Underworld."

"You? Seriously? But how?"

"How else?" replies Mathena. "With math!"

"HUZZAH! WE ARE SAVED!" cries Deadipus. "Wait—did you just say, 'With *math*'?"

Mathena takes this crazy-looking doohickey out of her bag. "I made this before we left. I call it a sextant—it's a doubly reflecting navigation instrument that measures the angular distance between an astronomical object and the horizon for the purposes of celestial navigation. I can estimate latitude by calculating angle with time of day, and measure lunar distance with another celestial object to determine Greenwich Mean Time and, therefore, longitude. Understand?"

Whoa! What happened? Must have dozed off for a bit! I see Mathena taking measurements and writing them down on the munched-up map.

"Mathena, can you really do this?" I ask.

"Yes, I can," Mathena replies.

"And can you tell what those arrows with DANGER!, AVOID!, and BEWARE! mean?"

"No, I can't."

(I should've stopped at "Yes, I can.")

"So," I ask, "when do you think we'll reach that DANGER! arrow?"

"By my calculations, I'm figuring . . . right now."

"Is that what your sextant thingy is saying?"

"No, that's what my eyes are saying," Mathena replies. "LOOK!!!"

CHAPTER 17

"**W**hat the heck is that?" I ask.

"Either he's got another eye in the back of his head, or that's a Cyclops!" replies Mathena. "I've read about them—they're very fond of boats!"

"Oh," I say. "What's so bad about that?"

"They like to eat them!" replies Mathena.

"Oh. That's bad." No one else is saying anything (a huge one-eyed giant will do that to you), so finally I look up at him and splutter, "Umm . . . h-h-h-hello, sir. Will you p-p-please let us p-p-pass?"

"WHY???" thunders the creature.

"Because we need to get by you?" I reply.

"WHY?"

"We're on our way to the Underworld," I say.

"WHY?"

"To find my uncle Hades."

"*Our* uncle Hades," Adonis chimes in.

"WHY?"

"To bring him back to Mount Olympus, where we live."

"WHY?"

"We . . . can't really tell you that."

"WHY?"

"It's a secret."

"WHY?"

"Our mother doesn't want anyone to know."

"WHY?"

"We . . . can't really tell you that, either."

"WHY?"

"What's with this dude?" mutters Gaseous. "Talk about a whysguy!"

Just when things couldn't get any worse, it starts sleeting—and we start sneezing! Then we look up and realize it's not sleet at all. The salivating Cyclops has wrapped a napkin around his neck, and he's grinding pepper on us! We're being seasoned!

"Achooo!!!" I sneeze. "Pardon me for asking this, but is 'Why?' all you can say?"

"WHY?"

"I'm curious."

"WHY?"

"I'd just like to know."

"WHY?"

"See? There you go again!"

"Oddonis, please—let me handle this," says Principal Deadipus, turning to the ogre. "I am Principal Deadipus of the Mount Olympus Middle School. If you do not let us pass, I'm afraid I will have to call your parents."

"WHY?"

"Because you are not allowing us to sail through!"

"WHY?"

"Only you can answer that question!"

"WHY?"

"BECAUSE YOU ARE THE ONE WHO IS OBSTRUCTING US!"

"WHY?"

"Oh, you are IMPOSSIBLE!" screams Deadipus.

Way to handle it, Principal D! Clearly, this is getting us nowhere. I turn to the beast and ask, "Could you excuse us for a minute?"

"WHY?"

"My friends and I need to talk things over."

"WHY?"

"Well, to be honest, you're kinda driving us crazy."

"WHY?"

"Never mind!"

"I figured it out, you guys," says Gaseous as we all huddle together. "That's not a Cyclops. That's a WHYCLOPS!"

CHAPTER 18

"Cyclops, Whyclops—either way, he's not letting us through!" I say. "What are we supposed to do?"

"The same thing Odysseus did to the Cyclops," answers Adonis. "Poke him in the eye!"

"Sounds good to me!" says Poseidon.

"Me too!" echoes Puneous.

"Me five!" adds Heracles.

"Have you seen the size of that Whyclops?"

"I can totally take him!" says Adonis.

"You???"

"Heracles can totally take him!" says Adonis.

I can already imagine how that'll turn out!

Hmmm.

"Maybe there's another way," I say. "Just follow my lead." I turn back to the Whyclops. "Tell me, Whyclops. What is the first letter in the word 'yo-yo'?"

"WHY?"

"That is correct! And what is the first letter in the word 'yellow'?"

"WHY?"

"RIGHT AGAIN!!! You're really good at this!"

"WHY?"

"Isn't it obvious? Because you're very, very smart!!!"

I whisper back to the crew, "Everybody think of Y words, and Heracles—start rowing!"

"What's the first letter in 'yak'?" asks Mathena.

"WHY?"

"GOOD!" we all cheer.

"Yogurt?" yells Puneous.

"WHY?"

"HOORAY!" we all yell.

"Yowza?" screams Gaseous.

"WHY?"

"Yodel?" hollers Poseidon.

"WHY?"

"Umm . . . errr . . . uhhh," mumbles Heracles.

We're almost through the Whyclops's legs! The only problem now is that the Whyclops is so excited that he's jumping up and down—and if one of his size-fifty feet lands on us, we're goners!

"How about 'YAY'?" we shout.

"And 'YES'?"

"WHY?"

"'YAHOO!!!'" I roar.

"WHY?"

"Why?" I call back. "I'll tell you why! Because we've sailed past you, Whyclops, and you can't get us anymore!"

"WHY?" the Whyclops moans.

"That's easy!" yells Mathena. "We're WHYS beyond our years!"

CHAPTER 19

"That. Was. TOTALLY AWESOME!!!" bellows Adonis.

"I can't believe we did that!" agrees Poseidon.

"WE ROCK!" echoes Puneous.

"OH, YEAHHHHHH!!!" roars Heracles.

Seriously??? WE??? If WE had followed my brother's plan, WE would be sailing through the Whyclops's small intestine right about now! And one more thing: what's with Puneous?

"Hey," I say to Puneous. "Why are you on the Gods' side? You're one of us!"

"Really?" hisses Puneous. "You sure didn't make me feel like that when you excluded me from this trip!"

Ouch. One more thing for me to feel guilty about. Puneous walks off in a huff. I'm hoping he'll get over it, though. After all, we just scored a major victory! Everyone's feeling relieved and excited after our close encounter of the one-eyed kind. Even Phaethon is pumped! He runs around the boat giving us all high fives.

Phaethon's always been a total downer, so I'm happy he's happy . . . until I realize that if he's high-fiving, then NOBODY'S DRIVING THE BOAT!

Thanks a lot, Phaethon! I'm about to utter a big "OH, NO!" but I'm shocked when an even bigger "OH, YES!!!" comes out of my mouth instead! See, we've run aground—right onto a beautiful beach! And it's not just any beautiful beach: it's a kid paradise!

We all pile out of the boat and make a beeline for the beach, but Principal Deadipus stops us.

"HALT! Stop right there, you ruffians! How dare you? Where are your manners? We are *guests* on this island, and representatives of Mount Olympus! We must exhibit civility! Decorum! Etiquette! Even in the face of unlimited sno-cones, bouncy castles, and hot tubs. Wait—HOT TUBS??? OUT OF MY WAY! LAST ONE IN IS A ROTTEN EGG!!!"

"Is this great or what?" asks Gaseous as we float in the perfectly heated pool. "Who ever thought a trip to the Underworld could be FUN?"

"Not me!" I reply.

Puneous paddles by, wearing the tiniest water wings ever. "Maybe we should skip the Underworld and stay here!"

Hmmm.

No! Mustn't . . . think . . . like that!

Mathena relaxes on a lounge chair, sunning herself while cuddling two cute piglets from the petting zoo. "This is the life," she sighs. "If only I had some calculus homework, too!"

"You've officially gone bananas," says Gaseous, peeling a banana. "In fact, you're nuts!" he adds, nibbling from a bowl of nuts.

"You know what's really nuts?" Mathena replies. "We haven't seen anybody else here! That banner says WELCOME TO MUMCE'S BEACH PARTY! So where's the party? And *who is Mumce?*"

The piglets start squealing like mad. They jump off Mathena's lounge chair and scurry away.

"Excellent questions, my child!" says a woman's voice. "*This* is your party, and *I* . . . am Mumce. But you may call me Mumzy Wumzy!"

We all turn our heads and there—standing by a frozen yogurt dispenser—is a dazzling enchantress.

"She's gorgeous!" Mathena whispers.

"You can say that again!" replies Gaseous. "And Mumce's pretty, too!"

CHAPTER 20

"**W**elcome, my children," says Mumce. "Enjoy my wondrous island. I made it just for you."

"Can do, Mumce!" says Gaseous, hoovering fro-yo straight from the machine. "Thanks!"

"Please," Mumce purrs. "Call me Mumzy Wumzy."

"Whatever you say, Mumzy Wumzy! Got any hot fudge?"

"Of course," says Mumce. "I've got EVERY-THING!"

Mumce's right: her beach BBQ is LIT! We're eating and drinking and dancing and playing and swimming and diving and snorkeling and mini-golfing and volleyballing and chilling like we've never chilled before! It's HEAVEN! As Adonis and I compete to see who can make the most *epic* frozen yogurt sundae of all time, Mumce sidles up next to us.

"Having a good time, kids?"

"This is the BOMB, Mumce!" says Adonis.

"Mumzy Wumzy," scolds Mumce.

"Oh, yeah—sorry, Mumzy Wumzy!"

"That's my good boy!"

"It's great, Mumzy Wumzy," I say. "I'm just sorry we have to leave!"

"Who says you have to leave? You can stay as long as you like!"

"Thanks," I reply. "But we've gotta go soon. We have to get to the Underworld."

"The *Underworld*?" Mumce says. "No, no, no—that's too dangerous for my babies!"

Okay, that's a little weird.

"The Underworld is no place for children! You belong here . . . with *me*."

Weirder.

"That's so nice of you, Mumzy Wumzy," I say.

"But we really can't stay."

"Oh, but you MUST!" replies Mumce. "Don't you understand? I built this island for YOU. Mumzy Wumzy wants to be a mommy. Mumzy Wumzy NEEDS to be a mommy. And you will all be Mumzy Wumzy's children . . . forever!"

WEIRDEST!

"Okaaaay, Mumzy Wumzy," I say. "Umm . . . we're going to have our yummy wummy sundaes now."

"Of course! Indulge yourselves, my precious angels! Your mommy just wants you to be happy!"

Mumce heads off to tend to her party, while Adonis and I start quietly passing the word: emergency meeting at the s'mores station!

"Listen up, you guys," I say. "We've got a problem."

"What problem?" replies Gaseous. "Too many s'mores???"

"I hate to say this, but Oddy's right," says Adonis. "Mumzy Wumzy is loony toony! She wants us to be her babies!"

"I'd be down with that!" says Gaseous.

"You won't be when you have to spend the rest of your life here, gasbag!" scoffs Adonis.

"So what are you proposing we do?" asks Mathena.

"What else?" replies Adonis. "Attack!"

"Sounds good to me," says Poseidon.

"Me too," echoes Puneous.

"Me six!" adds Heracles.

"Not again!" I moan. "Even you, Puneous?"

"Hey, we tried it your way with the Whyclops—"

"Yeah! And it worked!"

Mathena interrupts and suggests, "Why don't we ask Principal Deadipus what he thinks?"

"There's more of us than there are of her," says Adonis. "Just leave it to the big guys, *ladies*. We'll take care of Mumce before you're done with your s'mores."

"Boys." Mathena sighs.

"It could work, though, right?" I say. "Adonis's plan, I mean. After all, there *are* four of them, and Mumce's just—"

"Wree! Wree! Wree!"

I'm interrupted by three shrieking pigs—and one teeny-tiny piglet—hoofing their way back to the fire pit. Nothing odd about that, except for the fact that the pigs . . . ARE WEARING TOGAS! The leader of the pork stops right in front of me.

CHAPTER 21

"**W**itch is such a strong word," murmurs Mumce as she strolls in behind the pigs. "My sister Circe—now, *she's* a witch. I much prefer 'magic maker' or 'sorceress.' Or just plain old . . . MOM."

"What did you do, Mumce?" I ask.

"I taught these *naughty boys* a lesson: if you *act* pigheaded, you might end up *being* pigheaded!"

"My mother's gonna kill me," says Puneous Pig.

"So that's why there are pigs all over the island," Mathena says to Mumce. "You've done this before!"

"It's not *my* fault there are so many disobedient children in the world!" snaps Mumce. "I'm just trying to be the best mother I can be! And speaking of that, Mommy thinks it's time for all her little darlings to go beddy-bye. That is . . . unless you're going to be *pigheaded* about it."

Gaseous yawns loudly. "Not me, Mommy! I'm soooooo tired!"

"Us too, Mama!" says Mathena. "Right, Oddy?"

"I'M POOPED, MA!" I yawn, until Mathena elbows me in the ribs.

"Put a sock in it, Sleepy!" hisses Mathena. "Night night, Mumzy Wumzy!"

"Good night, my sweet petunias! Sleep tight! Don't let the pig lice bite!"

"Don't let the bedbugs bite" is bad enough—but *pig lice*???

Naturally, Mumce's bedrooms are as sumptuous as her barbecues. We've all got comfy king-size beds, fluffy robes and jammies, and a bounteous buffet of late-night snacks. But none of us has much of an appetite . . . well, almost none of us.

"Stop pigging out and listen up, you guys!" I whisper. "We've got to figure a way out of here!"

"May I squeak . . . umm . . . speak?" says Adonis.

It's pretty hard to take him seriously because his face, snout, and whiskers are smeared with chocolate.

"Sure, Pigasus—I mean, Adonis." I giggle.

"*Oink oink*, very funny," says Adonis. "Here's my new plan: I think we can take her!"

"That's the same as your old plan!" I wail.

"Sounds good to me," squeals Poseidon Pig.

"Me too," echoes Puneous Pig.

"Me eight!" grunts Heracles Hog.

"I think we've heard enough from the Four Little Pigs," I say.

"Are you sure they'll be okay out there?" asks Mathena. "What if they get cold?"

"Then we'll throw a blanket on them," replies Gaseous. "Mmmm—pigs in blankets."

"Don't worry about them—they're in hog heaven," I say. "Meanwhile, we're still up a creek."

"What are we supposed to do?" asks Gaseous. "Mumce's one wacky witch!"

"I've never seen anybody want to be a mom that bad," says Mathena.

"Mumce should talk to *my* mom," mutters Gaseous. "She says being a mother stinks!"

"She really says that???" asks Mathena.

"Yeah," replies Gaseous. "Especially after I've eaten beans!"

"Mumce should try babysitting my dad," I say. "That would change her mind real fast!"

Hmmm.

"Wait a second," I say. "That might be it!"

"What might be it?" asks Mathena.

"I've got a plan. Trust me—and do what I do."

"Should we tell the porkers?" asks Gaseous.

"Better not," I reply. "We wouldn't want them to SQUEAL on us!"

CHAPTER 22

Operation Mumce and Me commences bright and early the next morning. Gaseous, Mathena, and I tiptoe our way into Mumce's bedroom. We take a running start and launch ourselves onto our slumbering Mumzy Wumzy.

"WHAT THE—????" bellows our groggy mommy. "Oh, my . . . children, you startled me! You mustn't surprise Mumce like that!"

"I WANT PANCAKES! I WANT PANCAKES!" screams Gaseous.

"YUCK, MOMMY! No pancakes! Waffles!" I demand.

"It's not fair, Mommy! They ALWAYS get what they want!" whines Mathena.

"Do not!" Gaseous and I yell.

"Do too!" wails Mathena.

"Do not, crybaby!"

"MO-OM!" moans Mathena. "They're picking on me!"

"BABY NEEDS HER BOTTLE! WAH WAH, BABY!!!"

"MAKE THEM STOP, MUMZY WUMZY!!!"

"Please, children, please," pleads Mumce. "Mommy needs her coffee first."

"BUT WE'RE HUNGRYYYYYY!!!!!" we bawl.

"All right, all right," grumbles Mumce. "Mommy will take a shower, and then get your breakfast."

"We'll help you make breakfast, Mumzy Wumzy!" says Mathena.

"That would be *wonderful*, Mathena my love!

You go to the kitchen, and Mommy will be there lickety-split!"

"Can I go potty before you shower, Mommy?" asks Gaseous.

"Of course, sweet Gaseous!" replies Mumce. "Go right ahead."

Gaseous enters Mumce's bathroom, emerges a minute later, and announces, "Sorry, Mumzy Wumzy. I missed."

"Oh, great." Mumce sighs. "But not to worry, my darling. I'll take care of it. You just wait for Mommy in the kitchen."

"Okay, Mommy!" we shout. "See you soon! We'll time you!"

OMGs—we are so annoying! We head down to the kitchen, and when Mumce comes downstairs after her shower, she has another surprise waiting for her.

"What have you DONE???" shrieks Mumce.

"I made you breakfast, Mama!" chirps Mathena.

"Did not!" Gaseous and I gripe.

"Did too, Booger Brains!" snaps Mathena.

"SHE CALLED US A NAME, MUMZY WUMZY!!!!!"

"STOP STOP STOP!!!" Mumce groans. "I'M BEGGING YOU!"

"Are you mad at us, Mumzy Wumzy?" asks Mathena.

"No, no, dear." Mumce sighs. "Mommy has a splitting headache, that's all. Say, I have an idea. Why don't you three go out and play?"

"We want to play with YOU, Mumzy Wumzy!" I say. "All day!"

"EVERY DAY!!!" shout Gaseous and Mathena.

"That's . . . nice," replies Mumce. "You go play by yourselves now—"

"But Mommy—"

"PLAY!!!!!!!" screams Mumce at the top of her lungs.

"Okay, Mumzy Wumzy, if you say so," says Mathena, eyeing Gaseous and me with a devilish grin. "Let's play."

CHAPTER 23

So, we play...

And play...

And play...

After all that, Mumce looks like she's about to go off the deep end!

"MUMCE NEEDS TO LIE DOWN, ANGELS!!!"

But we've saved the best for last. We wait until Mumce is sound asleep, and then release the hounds . . . I mean, pigs!

"THAT'S IT! I'VE HAD IT!" cries Mumce. "I *HATE* BEING A MOTHER! CHILDREN ARE THE *WORST*!!!"

"Sorry, Mumzy Wumzy!" I say.

"We thought you liked pigs!" adds Mathena.

"I NEVER WANT TO SEE ANOTHER PIG IN MY LIFE!"

"Speaking of pigs . . . what's for dinner, Mumzy Wumzy?" asks Gaseous. "We're STARVING!"

"NOTHING'S FOR DINNER! YOU'RE LEAVING! NOW!!!!!!!"

"Are you sure, Mommy?" says Mathena.

"OH, I AM VERY SURE! ALL OF YOU—TAKE A HIKE!!!!"

With a flick of her wrist, Mumce undoes the spell and turns all the pigs back into their old annoying selves.

We quickly grab Principal Deadipus (he's still in the hot tub!) and skedaddle back to the *Greek Freak*. I've never been happier to see Phaethon in my life! We wave goodbye to our paradise lost—and to the mother we're glad we never had!

"BYE-BYE, MUMZY WUMZY!" we all yell.

"GOOD RIDDANCE, YOU HORRIBLE BRATS!" calls Mumce.

As we sail off into the sunset, Mathena, Gaseous, and I take a moment to give ourselves a much-deserved pat on the back.

"That. Was. AWESOME!" bellows Adonis.

"I can't believe we did it—again!" agrees Poseidon.

"WE ROCK!" echoes Puneous.

"OH, YEAHHHHH!!!" roars Heracles.

"Hogwash!" fumes Gaseous.

"I wish I could give them some credit," I seethe. "But that would be like putting . . . LIPSTICK ON A PIG!"

CHAPTER 24

After some serious shut-eye, Gaseous, Mathena, Principal Deadipus, and I wake up refreshed. Adonis, Poseidon, Heracles, and Puneous are still asleep, though—and it's pretty clear they're not quite used to being human again.

Also, you should've seen their faces at breakfast when we offered them a choice of bacon, ham, or sausage!

So here we are, back out on the high seas, awaiting our next adventure.

WE'VE MADE IT THROUGH "DANGER" AND "AVOID" BUT WE KNOW THAT "BEWARE" IS STILL OUT THERE...

In the meantime, there's some danger I've been avoiding that's right in front of me, and I can't put it off any longer. I search the boat for Puneous and find him sitting alone on the railing, looking out at the endless sea.

"It's so big," Puneous says. "And I'm so little. I don't think I've ever felt so small."

"You're not that small," I say.

"Don't lie," he says. "That's why you didn't ask me to come along with you. I'm useless."

"You're not useless," I say. "You're fearless!"

"Oh, please . . ."

"It's true. I'm sorry I didn't have the courage to tell you about this trip. You're my friend, and I owed you that. I'm sorry, Puneous. Can you forgive me?"

"Well, you did kinda save me from being a piglet for the rest of my life, so I guess we're almost even."

"Welcome back to the Odd side," I say.

"It's good to be back," replies Puneous. "It was fun being a God for a little while, but it wasn't really me. Also, I gotta say: those Gods sure are a bunch of hotheads!"

I smile, but don't say a word. Puneous and I scan the seas together, keeping our eyes open. The map says BEWARE but we don't see anything. Then suddenly, we *hear* something. It's very faint, far off in the distance, and we could so easily ignore it. But instead of steering *away* from the sound, Phaethon turns the wheel and starts heading *toward* it—and none of us stop him!

The closer we get, the more bewitching the sound becomes. It's a chorus of bings, booms, and bleeps—and it's the most mesmerizing sound any of us has ever heard!

"So bumpin'," murmurs Adonis.

"So thumpin'," mumbles Poseidon.

"So crumpin'," mutters Heracles.

"Bumpin'? Thumpin'? *Crumpin'*?" asks Mathena. "Have you all lost your bleepin' minds?"

We're getting near enough to see what's making the sound. It's a group of beautiful girls sitting on top of a rocky cliff! But nobody cares about that—because they are playing THE COOLEST VIDEO GAME EVER!

CHAPTER 25

It will probably come as no surprise that Adonis and I have very different tastes when it comes to video games. He's more of a shoot-'em-up guy—he loves games like *Fleecenite* and *Phobos V: Horror Hunter*. Me? I'm totally addicted to *Oddcraft*.

129

I'M A UNICORN
and I JUST MADE A HOUSE
OUT OF CHEESE! *yay!*

But this game these girls are playing . . . holy cow!
What design! What graphics! What interfaces! It's
gorgeous!

We're sailing closer and closer to the cliff every
second. But nobody seems to care!

"So jagged," I murmur.

"So dangerous," Puneous mumbles.

"So what," Gaseous mutters.

"Hello? What is wrong with you guys?" asks
Mathena.

It's the strangest thing—we know the *Greek Freak* is about to be dashed to bits, but we're powerless to do anything about it! We *must* find out who these girls are—and more importantly, what game they're playing!

"Who are you?" I call to them.

"The Sirens!" one of the girls says quickly. "Kinda

busy, though. We're totally schooling some Peloponnesian kids!!!"

"What is that awesome game you're playing?" begs Adonis.

"And can we get dibs on the next game?" asks Gaseous.

"Sure!" the girls reply. "It's called *Sirens IV: Titan War!*"

"Come closer to the rocks so we can teach you!" urge the Sirens.

"Full speed ahead, Heracles!" cries Adonis.

Heracles rows harder and harder. The cliff gets nearer and nearer. We're either being soaked by sea spray—or I just wet my toga.

"Umm . . . you guys did hear them say they're *Sirens*, right?" asks Mathena. "As in, lure-sailors-to-their-deaths Sirens? As in, don't you see how close we're getting to those rocks???"

"Yes!" screams Gaseous. "Isn't it great? We can really see the game now!"

Mathena turns to Principal Deadipus and says, "Can't you do something?"

"I can try," replies Principal Deadipus. "Now hear this!" he commands. "There will be no video games on this ship!"

I'LL PUT YOU ALL IN DETENTION!

NO RECESS FOR A YEAR!

I'LL SHAVE YOUR HEADS AND COVER YOU IN SOUR CREAM!!

"I should have known," Deadipus sighs. "We adults are powerless against the Siren song of video games."

"Check it out!" barks Poseidon. "One of the characters looks like Heracles!"

"How can me be there when me here?" yells Heracles. "Me confused!"

"You can choose whoever you want to be!" shouts one of the Sirens.

"My character is Enyo, Goddess of war," adds another. "I just broke out of prison in Tartarus, and now I'm looking for revenge! Join me!"

"Come playyyyy! Come playyyyy!" sing the Sirens.

"Okayyyyy! Okayyyyy!" we reply.

We're all completely hooked. Even Mathena looks psyched!

"Wow—this is great!" she exclaims.

"I'm so glad you feel that way!" I say. "What changed your mind?"

"Well," she replies, "I realized something: this game is all about *math*!"

TOTAL. SILENCE.

"What do you mean, it's about . . . *math*?" asks Adonis.

"I mean, it's as simple as two plus two!" she says. "If you like math, then you'll love this game!"

"B-b-but it's not a math game!" blubbers Adonis. "IS IT???"

"IT'S NOT! IT'S NOT!" shriek the Sirens.

"Sure it is!" raves Mathena.

"It's *TOTALLY* a math game! Come on! Do the math!"

CHAPTER 26

"This is a tough one!" groans Adonis. "You might even call it a . . ."

co·nun·drum
(ke-nun´drem)
noun
A confusing and difficult problem or question.

"Hey," I suggest. "Maybe we could play *Oddcraft* instead!"

"Okay, that settles it," grumbles Adonis. "We're leaving."

"NOOOOOOOO!!!" scream the Sirens.

"You heard him." Mathena smiles. "Adonis doesn't play math games."

"Pleeeeeease?" beg the Sirens. "Just one?"

"Sorry, sisters," replies Mathena. "Game over."

Whoa—talk about a game changer! Mathena's "Oh, snap!" snaps us out of the spell we were all under. Ever so carefully, we row past the Sirens' cliff, and out of harm's way.

"I'm very proud of you, children," says Principal

Deadipus. "I believe the phrase is . . . bad pops?"

"It's *mad props,* sir," I reply. "And thanks—but we couldn't have done it without Mathena."

"Quite right," says Deadipus. "Her actions were truly . . . *titanic!*"

CHAPTER 27

Phew! That was a close one! We've made it past the Whyclops, Mumce, and—thanks to Mathena's quick thinking—the Sirens!

Next stop: the Underworld!

An overwhelming feeling of dread settles over the crew of the *Greek Freak* when we pass an island and see this ominous sign:

"So, th-th-this is it," I stammer.

"I just remembered—I left my retainer at home! Can we t-t-turn around?" stutters Gaseous.

We sail on until we eye some figures standing on the shore, waving at our boat. We all shudder. What fiendish demons await us? What hideous ghouls might they be? I grab the spyglass, swallow hard, and prepare myself for the worst.

This is what we've been so afraid of? *This* is the inferno of eternal misery? *This* is the bottomless pit of doom? Two guys in tighty whities??? We row the boat to shore and slide up on the soft sand.

"Ahoy there, matey!" yells Poseidon. "Is this the Underworld?"

"Not quite!" one of them chuckles. "But you're getting warmer!"

"Well, where are we then?"

"This here . . . is UnderWEAR World!"

"Underwear World???" I ask.

"You betcha!" says his buddy. "Welcome, strangers! I'm Hanes—rhymes with Hades, but don't you worry, I'm not him! And that fella over there is Jockeyus! Now, first things first: if you'd be so kind, please recite the Underwear World pledge of allegiance. Everybody ready? Repeat after me! 'UNDERWEAR is FUN TO WEAR!'"

"Do we have to?" asks Puneous.

"Only if you want to live!" roars Jockeyus . . . gulp . . . jokingly?

"Hahaha," we answer nervously. "Uhhh . . . underwear is fun to wear?'"

"Good! That wasn't so hard, was it?" says Hanes. "All righty then, if you'll follow me, you lucky duckies are in for a treat! You have been summoned to meet the grand ruler of Underwear World himself!"

"And who might that be?" asks Principal Deadipus.

"Why, King Tightywhiteyus, of course!"

"Of course," says Deadipus.

Before exiting the boat, we gather together for a quick conference.

"What do you guys think we should do?" I ask.

"Okay, here's the thing," whispers Adonis. "Those dudes are only wearing undies. So *obviously* we should attack!"

"Sounds good to me," says Poseidon.

"Me . . . tutu," adds Heracles.

"We've done pretty well using diplomacy so far," I add. "Why stop now?"

"Because it's more fun to just attack?" replies Adonis.

"Violence will get you nowhere, Adonis," scolds

143

Principal Deadipus. "I say we try to be gracious guests, pay our respects to this King Tightywhit-eyus, and then be on our way."

We all agree to follow Deadipus's plan. And so we're off to see the prince of panties, the baron of briefs, the lord of lingerie . . .

. . . the duke of drawers! Okay, *now* I'm done.

CHAPTER 28

Hanes and Jockeyus lead us down a jungle path until we reach a clearing. Trumpets blare, and there—sitting on a throne—is King Tightywhiteyus.

"Greetings, travelers! Welcome to Underwear World! I am King Tightywhiteyus, son of King Thongous and Queen Tankinia . . ."

Principal Deadipus sees what's happening. He's been around kids long enough to know the old formula:

BOYS + UNDERWEAR = LAUGHTER

So he knows he's only got *seconds* until we all crack up. And the king's lineage sure isn't helping any!

"Grandson of King Skivvius and Queen Pantaloonia . . ."

"Your grace," interrupts Principal Deadipus. "It is an honor to meet you, and we thank you for your hospitality. As a token of our appreciation, I offer you my most treasured undergarments."

"Leaping long johns!" King Tightywhiteyus cries with delight. "A pair of woolies!"

"And now, your highness, we beg your pardon, but we are on a mission of great urgency. Therefore, we must unfortunately take our leave."

This does not go over well. The Underwearers all start murmuring to each other. I hear them whispering stuff like "Unbralievable!" and "Weren't they briefed?" and "I don't underwearstand!"

"Leave?" replies the king. "No, no, no, you can't!"

"I'm afraid we must, sire."

"You misunderstand me, sir. I don't mean 'You can't' like 'Oh, I wish you wouldn't!' I mean 'You can't' like 'No, YOU CANNOT!'"

"Whaddya mean, we CANNOT?" sneers Puneous.

"No one leaves Underwear World without learning our national dance!" says the king. "It's our gift to civilization! We call it the Undie. Trust me—you'll love it!"

Here's another tried-and-true kid formula:

BOYS + DANCING IN PUBLIC = HUMILIATION

"*DANCE???*" we all whimper.

"Yes indeed! In the underwear of our choice!" decrees the king.

"No way, pal!" roars Adonis. "Now you've gone too far!"

"King Tightywhiteyus . . . if we dance, then may we go?" asks Deadipus.

"Of course!" replies the king. "You have my word."

"Very well," says Deadipus. "My students and I shall confer."

"Here's *my* word," Adonis hisses to Deadipus. "Attack!"

"I don't like it any more than you do, Adonis," whispers Deadipus. "But remember what I said: violence will get you nowhere!"

Reluctantly, we do as Deadipus says . . . and the next thing you know, *this* is happening!

I hate to admit it, but once we get past the initial EXTREME embarrassment, doing the Undie is actually kind of fun! When the dance is over, Principal Deadipus shakes hands with King Tightywhiteyus and thanks him for including us in his panty party.

"That was unbelievable Undie-ing!" gushes the king. "Dance with us tomorrow, too!"

"I wish we could, your highness," says Deadipus. "But alas, we cannot."

"You misunderstand me again, sir," says the king.

"When I say, 'Dance with us tomorrow,' I don't mean 'Please!' I mean, 'You WILL dance with us tomorrow!'"

"But you said we could go!" replies Deadipus. "You gave us your word!"

"I did! And now I give you my word again—and that word is STAY!"

"That's . . . underhanded!" wails Deadipus.

"Not only that," brags the king. "It's . . . under-WEARhanded! Hahahaha!"

Deadipus gathers us all together and whispers, "All right, everyone, you heard the king."

"You mean we're staying?" I ask.

"No, I mean we're attacking!"

Mathena gasps. "But you said, 'Violence will get you nowhere!'"

"Violence *will* get you nowhere!" hisses Deadipus. "But *wedgies* will get us back on our boat!"

Here's another classic kid formula:

BOYS + OUTRAGE + UNDERWEAR = WEDGIES

"Now you're speaking our language, Deadly!" replies Adonis. "Let's get ready to . . . GRUNNNN-NNNNNNNDY!"

"NO MORE!" screams King Tightywhiteyus. "UNCLE!!!"

"Will you let us go?" says Principal Deadipus.

"YES! YES!" replies the king. "Will you promise to stop?"

"You have our word," says Adonis. "And that word is . . .

"WEDGIE!!!"

CHAPTER 29

When we're back onboard the *Greek Freak*, Adonis & Co. are even more insufferable than usual. So much high-fiving! So much chest bumping! So much woot wooting! They're all strutting around like a bunch of . . .

"We came. We saw. We wedgied," brags Adonis.

"Wedgie tsunami!" gloats Poseidon.

"Walkin' in a Wedgie Wonderland!" sings Heracles.

"You know what I always say, boys," crows Adonis. "Might is right! Now, BRING ON THE UNDER-WORLD!!!"

Suddenly the sky begins to darken. The sea begins to churn. The wind begins to howl. And I begin to panic!

BOOM!!! goes the thunder.

CRASH!!! goes the lightning.

GURGLE!!! goes my stomach.

The *Greek Freak* gets tossed around like one of Trianus's chew toys. Hurricane-force gales batter the boat, and giant swells push us along toward a dark tunnel that looms ahead. Mathena desperately tries to calculate angles that Phaethon can use to steer us out, but it's no use. Even the Gods fail! Poseidon thrusts his trident at the roiling sea to try to calm it, and Heracles paddles with all his might, but they're powerless against the savage storm.

"I *really* need my retainer, you guys!" screams Gaseous. "Let's turn back!"

A monster wave slams into our boat from behind and hurls us into the tunnel. In an instant, everything goes black . . . *and* gets really, really HOT.

I whisper into the darkness, "Is everybody okay?"
PFFFFFFFFFFFFTTTTTTTTTTT!!!!!!

"Again, Gaseous," murmurs Principal Deadipus, "a simple 'yes' would suffice!"

"Anybody got a light?" Puneous asks.

"I do!" replies Adonis.

He whips out the fire stick that Hestia gave Dad for his birthday—the same fire stick Dad told him *not* to play with! Adonis glares at me and says, "Hey, I sure wasn't gonna let Zeusy have it!"

For once I'm glad my brother never listens! The fire stick fills the tunnel with a warm glow. As we float along the water—which has narrowed to

a sliver of river—we can see signs hanging off the walls.

Yep, exactly what I was afraid of. We're officially in the Underworld . . . and I'm officially freaking out!

CHAPTER 30

We drift deeper and deeper into the tunnel. Steam rises off the river. The water is so hot that it's starting to bubble! Oh, and here's a nice touch: it reeks of rotten eggs!

"Ahhhh," sighs Gaseous. "Smells like home."

This is why I don't have sleepovers at Gaseous's! The one good thing about the horrible odor is that it helps me not think about how scared I am. I'm so petrified I can barely move. Then I look around at my friends. Come Hades or high water, they're still here! They didn't have to come along with Adonis and me. They all knew how dangerous this journey could be, and they came just the same. And none of them are abandoning ship now. Well, I say to myself, if they can keep going, I guess I can, too!

"*SQUAWWWWKKK!*" cries Penelope Pigeon from high up in the crow's nest.

I think she's spotted something! Off in the distance, another sign begins to emerge through the fog of steam.

"Does anyone have any cash?" asks Principal Deadipus.

Seriously, Principal D??? I know teachers are underpaid, but this is too much. You're the grown-up here!

Meanwhile, someone—or some*thing*—is standing on the dock waiting for us.

That must be Charon—the ferryman of the dead! It's weird, but I feel like I've seen him somewhere before!

"Cash or U-Pass?" he grunts.

"What's a U-Pass?" I say.

Charon sighs. (I'm guessing he has to answer this question a lot.)

"U-Pass gets you rides on all the rivers of the Underworld: the river of pain, river of forgetfulness, river of fire, river of wailing, and river of hatred."

"I think we'll pass on the U-Pass," I reply.

"We're here to see Hades," says Adonis. "He's our uncle."

"River Styx, then," grumbles Charon. "Cash only. Pets half-price. Dead guy free."

"I beg your pardon!" snorts Principal Deadipus. "I am very much alive!"

"Umm . . . Mr. Charon, sir?" I squeak. "We don't have any money."

Charon glares at me, heaves a huge sigh, and growls, "I am Charon, son of Erebus and Nyx. It is my duty to ferry the souls of the deceased over the River Styx in the service of my master, Hades. My payment is a coin that is placed in the mouth of the corpse. It's a dirty job, but somebody has to do it. No coin, no ride."

Adonis turns to all of us and whispers, "Anybody up for an attack?"

Then, from the back of the boat, we hear a voice say, "I got this." Phaethon steps forward, turns to Charon, and mutters mournfully, "I'm Phaethon, the driver. My father is Helios, the Sun God. He granted me one wish, and I asked to drive his sun chariot across the sky. He said it would be too much for me. I said it wouldn't be, but it was, and I crashed. As punishment, I'm doomed to drive a school chariot for all eternity."

Charon replies, "You have to drive a *school chariot* for all eternity?"

Phaethon nods and moans, "For all eternity."

"Wow," Charon exclaims. "That's even worse than my job!"

"Trust me," Phaethon says, sighing. "It is."

"Well, I'm still going to need *some* form of payment," says Charon. "Got anything else on board?"

Hmmm.

The only other things we have are . . . are . . . hold on . . . wait a minute . . . oh my Gods . . . that's it! That's where I've seen Charon before! The only other things we have on board . . . are THESE!

"Awww—they're adorable!" gushes Charon.

"These cutie patooties will work!" Charon cries. "All aboard!!!"

Mom was right—the trolls are good luck! Everyone (including the pets) disembarks from the *Greek Freak* and climbs into Charon's rickety boat. It's hard to believe we're actually feeling *lucky* that we get to cross the river of death. Then again, nothing about this trip is surprising me anymore!

CHAPTER 31

"**W**elcome aboard the Styx Shuttle," drones Charon. "Please stow your carry-on bags in the compartment below you and keep your seat backs and tray tables in the upright and locked position. Also, keep your hands, arms, legs, feet, wings, paws, and tails inside the boat at all times. In the event of a water emergency, it really won't matter because you're already on the river of death. In a moment, I'll be coming through the cabin to offer refreshments. Today's choices are blood of the damned and mini pretzels."

I wasn't expecting much, but the Styx Shuttle has to be the worst way to travel *ever*. The eerie darkness, the smell of sulfur, and the stifling heat are overwhelming. The constant wailing of the departed souls is terrifying. And Charon's tour is an absolute NIGHTMARE.

"Coming up on your left are grief, war, anxiety, diseases, and old age. On your right are fear, hunger, death, agony, and eternal sleep."

"This is freaking me out, dude," Gaseous hisses to me. "Plus, these pretzels are stale!"

"Try the blood of the damned," whispers Deadipus. "It's spicy!"

It gets worse, though. Charon rattles on as we pass some of the most hideous and horrifying creatures I've ever seen!

GORGONS!

THE CHIMERA!

THE LERNAEAN HYDRA!

AND WORST OF ALL...

THE SUBSTITUTE TEACHER!

"MAKE IT STOP!" screams Puneous.

Finally, after what seems like an eternity, Charon's boat slows and the hellish ride is over.

"It's been our pleasure scaring you today," says Charon. "As you exit, please fill out your comment cards and let us know how we can make your next visit less enjoyable."

We file out of Charon's boat, and there—rising up before us—stand the Gates of Hades. Yikes! On the gates is a huge sign with three ominous words: BEWARE OF DOG.

Double yikes! We all know what monstrous mutt *that* is: CERBERUS!!!

"How are we supposed to get past him???" asks Mathena.

"Beats me," replies Charon. "You could try offering him the smallest member of your group as a sacrifice while the rest of you go through!"

"WHY THE SMALLEST???" roars Puneous.

"He likes small plates," replies Charon. "Easier for him to digest."

Puneous glares at us and says, "You're not actually CONSIDERING this, are you???"

Hmmm.

Before I can answer, Cerberus starts creeping toward us, his three heads snorting and slobbering and sniffing the air like he's closing in on an all-you-can-eat buffet! Fiery, foul dog breath mingles with the rotten-eggy air. Trust me: no one will EVER make a candle called Underworld Potpourri. Still, the stench does attract one member of our crew: TRIANUS!

"NOOOOO!!!" I howl. "STAY, BOY, STAY!!!"

But it's a dog-meet-dog world out there! Trianus bounds past me and hightails it toward Cerberus—until he comes face-to-face with the heinous hellhound. Correction: make that FACES-TO-BUTTS!

"Okay, *I get it*," Gaseous observes. "But it's still disgusting."

"Stop staring and start sprinting, you guys!" orders Mathena. "This is our chance! Cerberus isn't guarding the gates!"

"She's right!" says Adonis. "He's busy mooning over Trianus! Let's go!"

"But I can't just leave him!" I sob.

"We'll call for him when we get through!" says Mathena. "Come on!"

We make a mad dash for the gates. But the gates are locked!

"What do we do?" I wail. "The gates are too narrow for us to squeeze through!"

"Too narrow for you chunky monkeys," says Puneous. "But not too narrow for me!"

Puneous climbs through and opens the gates from the other side!

"So," I say to Puneous, "who were you saying was *useless* again?"

In all the excitement, I almost forget about Trianus! I whistle for my plucky pooch, and he comes running, too. I wait for Cerberus to give chase, but from the looks of things, it appears the sniff-a-thon has soothed the savage beast!

Hey, you know what they say: LOVE STINKS!

CHAPTER 32

Trianus makes his escape from Cerberus's lovesick snouts, and we bolt the gates behind us.

We turn around to find a huge frosted-glass door in front of us.

"I wonder what *that* means," says Gaseous.

"Should we go in?" I ask.

"What choice do we have?" replies Mathena. "There's no going back now!"

We open the door and step into an empty waiting room with gray linoleum floors, gray plastic chairs, and buzzing fluorescent lighting. It looks a lot like a dentist's office—which, to a bunch of kids, is not exactly reassuring!

We approach the frosted-glass windows and press a small white button that rings way too loudly. The window panels slide open and the receptionists angrily bark, "Can I help you???"

Wow—what Harpies! And by that I mean ACTUAL HARPIES!

"H-h-hello," I sputter. "My name is Oddonis. We're here to see Hades, please."

"He's our uncle," adds my brother. "And I'm Adonis—maybe you've heard of me? I'm kind of a big deal."

The Harpies ignore Adonis and squawk, "Do you have an appointment?"

"N-no," I reply. "But it's really important that we see him. We've come a long way."

"It's the Underworld, sweetie," they sneer. "Everybody's come a long way. Take a seat and we'll call you when it's your turn."

The Harpies slam the windows shut. The only thing we can do is sit and wait. And wait. And wait.

Like the rest of the Underworld, Hades's waiting room is boiling hot. The chairs are hard and uncomfortable. The constant buzzing of the lights is beyond annoying. And the WORST SONG is playing over the tinny-sounding speakers. Plus, the song keeps *repeating* over and over and over!

It's like this place was specially designed to drive us crazy!

"I can't take it anymore!" hisses Adonis. "I gotta get outta here!"

"Oh, yeah?" I tease. "What are you going to do—bust down the door?"

"Now you're talking!" replies Adonis.

"Sounds good to me," says Poseidon.

"Me . . . forget what come next," says Heracles.

"Arrrggghhh!" I moan. "Not again!"

"This isn't Underwear World, you guys," says Mathena. "It's the Underworld!"

I plead with Puneous, "Can you talk to these knuckleheads?"

"Sorry," replies Puneous. "I don't speak Moron anymore."

"Line up!" says Adonis to his crew. "Assume battering ram positions!"

"Three! Two! One!" counts Adonis. "GO!!! RAMMING SPEEEEED!!!!"

The Three Dunceketeers smash through the waiting-room door, and all we hear is a collective cry of *"AAAAHHHHHHHH!!!"* as they disappear into a dark and fiery abyss!

The glass panels slide open again, and the Harpies announce, "The God of the Underworld will see you now."

Hmmm.

After seeing what I just saw, I'm not sure I want to be seen! See?

"Do we have to go?" asks Gaseous. "I forgot to mention, I'm allergic."

"Allergic to what?" I ask.

"DYING!!!"

"Like it or not," I sigh, "we have to go after those idiots." I peer into the pitch-black abyss on the other side of the door, turn to Mathena, and say, "Ladies and poultry first?"

"Please. After you," she replies. "We insist."

I take a deep breath, step through the doorway, and

SLIDE

DOWN

DOWN

DOWN

FARTHER

AND

FARTHER

AND

FARTHER!

It's like the world's longest, darkest, fieriest, creepiest playground slide ever!

I land with a *THUD* on the floor of a cave, and then everyone else lands with a *THUD THUD THUD THUD THUD THUD THUD THUD* on top of me!

"ODDY! HELP! GET US OUT OF HERE!" cries my brother. But where is my brother? I hear him, but I don't see him!

"LOOK UP!" yells Poseidon.

Here's a handy tip: whenever you hear "HELP!" followed by "LOOK UP!"—it's not good!

"What are we supposed to do?" I ask. "You're in a steel cage hanging over a lava pit!"

"Right! And it's all your fault!" spews Adonis.

"*MY* fault?" I cry. "How do you figure that? *I'M* not the one who keeps leaping before he looks!"

"Well, we wouldn't be here if you hadn't turned Dad into a toddler!"

"I didn't do that! Hades did that!"

"With your help, *brozo*!"

"Hey, you chose to come along on this trip!" I say. "I didn't make you!"

"Well, *you'd* still be doing the Undie with Tightywhiteyus if it weren't for me!"

"Oh, please, don't get me started—"

Our catfight is interrupted by a loud and sinister laugh that echoes through the colossal cavern.

"HAHAHAHAHA!" the voice booms. "PLEASE KEEP GOING! IT'S LIKE A TRIP DOWN MEMORY LANE!"

"Who said that?" asks Adonis.

"YOU SOUND JUST LIKE YOUR FATHER AND ME WHEN WE WERE YOUR AGE!" thunders the voice.

It's HADES! He's here! He's there! He's . . . EVERYWHERE! Oh my Gods, this is it! The moment we've all been waiting for!

From out of the shadows, Hades slowly emerges.

Wow—sure wasn't expecting that!

"Well, well, well," murmurs Hades. "You made it. Hello, nephews."

"H-h-hi, Uncle H-H-Hades," I stammer. "Long time no see."

"Oddonis," Hades says, looking me over. "My, my, my. So grown-up."

"What about me?" Adonis shouts from his cage. "Have I grown up?"

"*Physically*, yes, Adonis," replies Hades. "But *emotionally*, not so much. Why do you think you and your impetuous friends are up there? You're just like your dear old dad—or, should I say, your dear *young* dad?"

"We need to talk to you about that, Uncle Hades," I say.

"Of course we do. But first, I want to spend time with my nephews and meet all your friends. No one ever visits me! We'll have dinner together, and then you'll stay for the night. You all look like you could use a *long, long rest*."

One more handy tip: whenever you hear "a long, long rest" and you're in the UNDERWORLD, that's not good, either!!!

CHAPTER 34

Hades tells us to freshen up before dinner.

FRESHEN UP WHAT?

MY BREATH?

MY PITS?

MY FEET?

I'm certainly not going to *ask* anyone because they probably know *exactly* what to freshen up and I'll look like a loser! I just stare into the bathroom mirror until Mathena knocks on the door and says, "Done freshening up?"

"You bet!" I say with *way* too much excitement. "So fresh! Really fresh! Pretty much everything on me is all freshened up!"

"I'm fresh as a daisy!" adds Gaseous.

"Will you two focus, please?" says Mathena. "We've got to figure out how to get Hades up to Olympus!"

"Yeah, but how are we going to do that?" whines Gaseous. "In case you hadn't noticed, Hades is a *God*! And Adonis, Poseidon, and Heracles are all locked in a cage!"

"Gaseous is right," I say. "Without their powers, we're nothing."

"Are you kidding?" cries Mathena. "Have we been on the same odyssey? Did those guys help us get past the Whyclops? Or Mumce? Or the Sirens? Or King Tightywhiteyus? NO!!! Well, Tightywhiteyus *maybe*, but other than giving some wicked wedgies, the Gods have been totally useless!"

"Hey, Mathena's right!" shouts Gaseous. "We Odds beat the odds!"

That's when—

"Wait! You know who else is odd?" I say. "Hades! Think about it! He's always been an outcast. That's why he's down in the Underworld while his brother is up on Mount Olympus!"

"So what's your point?" asks Mathena.

"We'll never force Hades to undo the spell he put on my dad. He's too proud, and too stubborn. But maybe we can trick him into doing it!"

"How?"

"I don't know," I reply. "But I do know that he needs to trust us first. We need to show Hades that he's an Odd, *just like us*—and that we like him *because* of his oddness, not despite it!"

A loud GONG sounds, calling us to dinner. As we make our way there, Principal Deadipus claps his skeletal hand on my shoulder and says, "A wise and mature suggestion, Oddonis. It turns out youth is *not always* wasted on the young!"

I'm not exactly sure what Deadipus's old-guy words mean, but some of them definitely stick in my brain.

"Wise . . . mature . . . youth . . . young . . ."

Humongous hmmm!

CHAPTER 35

We creep back into Hades's cavern, where a long dining table has been set with all sorts of fancy plates and silverware. Lit candles cover the dark cavern walls, and organ music plays in the background. Super spooky!

189

But not as spooky as the menu!

Menu
Filet of Soul
Stuffed Ghost Peppers
Death by Chocolate

"I think I lost my appetite," whispers Gaseous.

"Welcome to my humble home, dear friends and family," says Uncle Hades.

"It's *beautiful*, sir," chirps Mathena. "So cozy, and stylish, and warm—"

"It's warm, all right!" calls Adonis from above. "LIKE AN OVEN!"

"Please ignore him, sir," Mathena says. "He has no taste."

"You really like it?" asks Hades excitedly. "Most of my guests don't. They think it's strange!"

"WELL, THAT'S A SHOCKER!" shouts Adonis.

"I really love my glassware," says Hades. "Don't you, Principal Deadipus?"

"I've missed you, Uncle Hades," I say. "Why don't you come to visit us anymore? Is it too far?"

"Heavens no, Oddonis," replies Hades. "I can travel wherever I want with a snap of my fingers! I just say where I'm going, and *bang*—I'm there!"

"Really?" I ask.

"You don't say!" adds Mathena.

"One snap!" says Hades. "No, the reason I never visit is simple: my brother hates me!"

"I can relate to that," I say.

"Oh, boo-hoo!" fake-sobs Adonis.

"It wasn't always that way." Hades sighs. "Zeus

and I were best friends when we were little. He was actually very sweet! But then he got power—and that was the end of that."

"He *is* sweet!" I say. "Well, sometimes, at least. That's what's been so great about your spell! It's like having a brother I actually get along with!"

"I heard that!" yells Adonis. "Hell-*oooooo*! What is wrong with all of you? Why are you making nice with this guy? You're all so odd!"

"He's got a point, Uncle Hades," I say. "We do have a lot in common."

"Hmmm," says Hades. "It's true. I've always been a bit of a misfit. Nobody understands me, or acknowledges me—especially my brother. But I'm important. I'm a God!"

"Yeah!" mocks Adonis. "GOD OF THE *DEAD*!"

Hades sighs. "That's what they all say. But death is a part of life! And death makes life more precious! Why can't anyone see that?"

"I see it, Uncle Hades," I say. "And I think it's cool. In an odd sort of way."

"I see it, too, sir," echoes Mathena. "What you said about life and death really adds up!"

"Abso-*PFFFFFF*ing-lutely!" toots Gaseous. "For a guy who lives in the Underworld, you're pretty chill, Hades. You're like one of us! You're not just a God . . . you're an Odd God!"

"I think I'm gonna be sick!" groans Adonis.

"Thank you," Hades says humbly. "It is nice to be appreciated, for once."

"And speaking of appreciated, how about that birthday poem Hades wrote to cast his spell on Zeus?" I say to everyone. "Was that brilliant or what?"

"It was clever, wasn't it?" grins Hades.

"Clever?" Mathena gasps. "It was genius!"

"Totes, dude!" adds Gaseous. "You make Homer sound like a gomer!"

"I just wish I could remember it!" says Mathena. "How'd it go again?"

"I think I remember!" I reply. "Wasn't it . . .

"And for your happy birthday treat,
I here perform this childish feat,
From here on out a kid you'll be,
And act like you're a wee baby!"

"No, no, no!" Hades laughs. "But very close! It's—

"And for your happy birthday gift,
You'll hereby make this boyish shift,
From here on out, a child you'll be,
And act as though you're only three!"

A bolt of lightning crackles inside the cavern, followed by a clap of thunder! Hades's lair fills with dense smoke. The fog is so thick that I can't see my hand in front of my face!

"Is everyone okay?" I cough.

"BLRRRRRRRRRRRRRTTTTT!!!!"

"WHY CAN'T YOU EVER JUST SAY 'YES,' GASEOUS???" cries Deadipus.

The smoke clears, and it appears we're all fine. Everyone, that is, but Hades. He wipes his nose, blinks his eyes, and whimpers to Mathena and me:

"MAMA? DADA? HADES NO LIKE BOOM BOOM!!!"

"**Y**ou did it, Oddy!" cries Mathena.

"WE did it!" I reply.

"What were you trying to do???" screams Adonis.

"HAHA!" cackles Gaseous. "Having clueless Gods around helps, too!"

"Well played, my boy," Principal Deadipus says to me.

"Awww! Thanks, Principal D," I say.

"YAY FOR DADA!" squeals Hades.

"I'm not your dada, Hades." I chuckle. "But I am part of your family. And you know who else is? That guy up there! Adonis!"

"YUCK!" scowls Hades. "ADONIS POOPY HEAD!"

"He can be." I smile. "But he's okay . . . sometimes."

"Gee, thanks a lot!" sulks Adonis.

"And you know who else is okay?" I tell Hades. "Your brother, Zeusy!"

"ZEUSY!" Hades gasps. "ME LOOOVE ZEUSY!"

"Do you want to *see* Zeusy?" Mathena asks Hades.

"YEAH YEAH! SEE ZEUSY! SEE ZEUSY! SEE ZEUSY!!!!"

With Little Hades's approval, we're able to lower Adonis and the rest of the captives down from their precarious perch. Then we all gather together in a circle around my underage uncle.

"Ready, Hades?" I say. "Just yell 'Zeusy's house' and snap your fingers!"

"OKEY DOKEY SMOKEY!" cries Little Hades. "BUT HOW YOU SNAP?"

Oh, geez. Ever teach a kid how to snap his fingers? It's not easy! But finally, after a long and frustrating tutoring session—and a lot of snack time—Little Hades finally gets it. We're ready for takeoff!

None of us has any idea what's about to happen—but we all agree that it's gotta be better than going back the way we came!

"Okay, Hades," Mathena whispers encouragingly. "Say 'Zeusy's house,' and then snap Mr. Fingers! One . . . twooo . . . threee . . ."

"ZEUSY'S HOUSE!"

"WHOAAAAAAAAAAAAAAAAAAAAA!!!!"

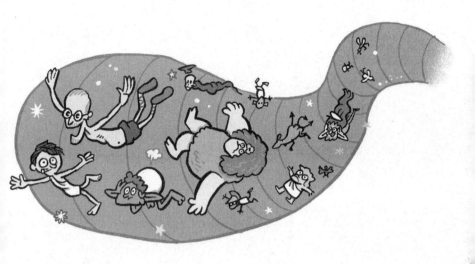

This is how my uncle travels????
POOF!!!

I open my eyes and we've landed—right in the middle of my living room!

My mom and my aunts scream, "THANK GODS! YOU'RE BACK!!!"

Hades takes one look at them and screams, "HI, SISTIES! HI, MAMA!"

Mom's excitement quickly evaporates.

"Oh, great," she moans. "Another one!"

CHAPTER 37

I don't think I've ever been hugged and kissed and squeezed so much in my entire life. Everyone is as happy to have us back as we are relieved to be back! It takes time for us to unwind—and for my cheeks to stop hurting from being pinched so hard—before we can begin to tell the story of our incredible *odd*yssey. Luckily, Zeusy is upstairs napping, and Hestia and Demeter are entertaining the King of the Underworld with a sock puppet.

"I can't believe you were able to trick Hades like that!" Mom exclaims.

"Hey, I did what I had to do!" brags Adonis.

I??? I . . . I . . . ¡Ay yi yi!

"Well, I think it's amazing, Adonis," Mom says. "You did all that, AND you brought everyone home safe and sound? Including your brother? Takk skal du ha, kjære. Thank you for taking such good care of him!"

"Oh, it was nothing," Adonis replies.

"So how is Hades going to reverse the spell?" asks Mom excitedly.

"Uhhh . . . good question," Adonis hems and haws. "But that's Oddy's department. How is Hades going to reverse the spell, *Oddy?*"

"Umm . . . I . . . guess I hadn't thought about that part," I say.

Mom gasps. *"You hadn't thought about that?!?"*

"Yeah, you hadn't thought about that?!?" echoes Adonis.

"No—but Hades is so psyched to see Dad," I protest. "Isn't that great?"

"Well, Dad won't be psyched to see Hades, I can tell you that!" Mom argues. "Have you heard the way your father talks about his brother?"

"Yes, but—"

"But nothing!" snaps Mom. "We could be looking at Trojan War II right here in this house!"

"Nice going, Oddy," hisses Adonis.

Just then, we hear a loud yawn from upstairs, followed by, "ZEUSY UP! ZEUSY COME DOWN NOW!!!"

Hades's ears perk up. "ZEUSY?"

"Oh nei," mutters Mom. "Oh nei, oh nei, oh nei . . ."

Next, we hear footsteps slowly coming down the stairs. *CLOMP. CLOMP. CLOMP.* It's like a horror movie! With every step, my whole body tenses. My aunts hold each other tight, their hands clapped over their mouths. Mom is covering her eyes and peeking through her fingers. And Hades is bobbing up and down and hopping from foot to foot like he has to pee! Finally Zeusy appears in the doorway, hair tousled, still rubbing the sleep out of his eyes. He yawns again, looks up at all of us, sees Little Hades, and . . .

"HADEY?"

"ZEUSY?"

The two brothers toddle toward each other, until they're almost nose to nose. They cock their heads at one another like puppies.

"HADEY WADEY!" chirps Zeus.

"ZEUSY WOOSY!" squeals Hades.

"Hadey Wadey mad at Zeusy Woosy?" asks Zeus.

"Hadey Wadey not mad at Zeusy Woosy," Hades replies. "Hadey Wadey LOVE Zeusy Woosy! Zeusy Woosy mad at Hadey Wadey?"

"Zeusy not mad!" Zeus cries. "Zeusy LOVE Hadey!"

Dad and Hades stare at each other. They blink, they gulp, and finally . . . THEY HUG!!!

ARE YOU KIDDING ME? ALL BECAUSE OF
A HUG???

The smoke clears, and Dad and Hades are staring
at each other again—but not in a good way.

"HADES!"

"ZEUS!"

"OUT OF MY HOUSE!" Dad roars.

"WITH PLEASURE!" Hades bellows. "TO THE UNDERWORLD!"

Hades is just about to snap his fingers when, out of nowhere, a voice thunders, **"STOP! STOP RIGHT THERE! BOTH OF YOU! DON'T. YOU. MOVE!!!"**

I look around the room, turn to Gaseous, and whisper, "Who said that?"

"Uhhh . . . ," Gaseous replies. "That was you, dude."

CHAPTER 38

Wait! That was *me*??? Oh, yeah! You're darn right that was me! I'm mad! I'm talking Minotaur-in-a-maze mad! Puneous-in-a-slam-dunk-contest mad! I'm FURIOUS!

"Listen, you two—we didn't make it through the Whyclops and Mumce and the Sirens and Underwear World *and* the Underworld to watch you do this!" I scold. "Didn't you hear yourselves a minute ago? You said you loved each other! What happened?"

"We grew up," says my dad.

"It's complicated," says my uncle.

208

"But it's not complicated!" I shout. "You're family! Of course you're going to bug each other! But deep down, you really do love each other! We all just saw it! And isn't that what matters most?"

"I don't know," Dad mumbles.

"Me neither," Hades grumbles.

"Look," I say. "My brother once told me, 'We're Gods. We fight. That's what we do.' Well, call me Odd, but I think there's more to being a God than that. If you're a God, you've got to be GODLY, too! You know—like, GOOD! Both of you were good when you were little. Then you got big and messed it all up! So why don't you stop acting like grown-ups and start behaving like children again?"

Ever so slowly, like two wary porcupines, Dad and Hades scowl, shrug, sigh, and at long last, smile.

"We'll try," they say together.

"FFFLLLLLLPPPPP FFFLLLLLPPPPP POORAY!" booms Gaseous.

"That's what I call a formula for success!" adds Mathena.

"It's a pretty tall order," says Puneous. "But I think they can do it!"

"I'm so proud of all of you!" Mom cries. "And I'm so grateful for what you two boys did for your father and me—especially you, Adonis. You're my hero!"

"What did he do?" asks Dad.

"Oh, nothing much—just saved Olympus, that's all! I'll explain later . . . Zeusy!"

"If I may, Freya," interrupts Principal Deadipus, "I think there's something you should know. With the exception of some well-timed wedgies, the Gods did far more harm than good on this journey. And, to be perfectly honest, so did I. We are only here because of your son Oddonis and the rest of the Odd Gods. It was their quick thinking, their ingenuity, and their diplomacy skills that saved the day . . . and Olympus."

"Is that true, Oddonis?"

"Umm . . . well . . . everybody helped, Mom," I reply.

"Adonis?" she says, turning to my brother.

211

Then Mom shakes out her arms and rotates her head. She closes her eyes, clears her throat, and . . . oh, man, look out . . . it's Thunder Mother time again!

Adonis is shivering in his sandals—just like the rest of us!

"Uhhh . . . not everybody, Mom," Adonis blubbers softly.

"Louder, please!" Mom thunders. "So everyone can hear you."

"I said, 'Not everybody helped.' I wouldn't be acting very godly if I said I did it," Adonis admits. "Because I didn't help. Not really. Oddy did most of it."

Whoa! What did he say???

"And what exactly did Oddonis do???" rumbles Mom.

Adonis sighs deeply. "He got us *out of* trouble," he declares. "I just got us *into* trouble. I thought power meant being, y'know, POWERFUL! But that didn't work so great this time. Oddy, Mathdweeba, Windbreaker, and Grumpy taught me the power of using your *brains*, instead of your fists."

"Don't forget the power of wedgies," I say.

"Right." Adonis smiles. "Anyway, it was the Odds that made things even. Those guys are the real heroes."

"Wow . . . thanks, Adonis," I say. "You're not going to hug me, are you?"

"Hey," Adonis replies, "if Dad and Hades can do it, I guess we can, too."

Here we go again!

Oh, no . . .

THE UNDERWORLD